THE UNEXPURGATED ADVENTURES OF

SHERLOCK HOLMES

BOOK 12

THE ADVENTURE OF THE PSYCHEDELIC TREES

by NP Sercombe

The un-edited manuscript originally entitled *The Adventure of the Copper Beeches* written by Dr. John Watson and Sir Arthur Conan Doyle

Illustrations by Juliet Snape

EVA Books

This novel is entirely a work of fiction. The names, characters and incidents portrayed in it are the work of the author's and illustrator's imaginations. Any resemblance to actual persons, living or dead, events or localities, is entirely coincidental.

Published by EVA BOOKS 2021 – c/o Harry King Films Limited
1&2 The Barn
West Stoke Road
Lavant
n/r Chichester
West Sussex PO18 9AA

A CIP catalogue record for this book is available from the British Library.

ISBN 978-1-8381045-3-5 (Hardback)

Book layout & cover design by Clare Brayshaw.

Cover illustration by Juliet Snape.

Set in Bruce Old Style.

Prepared and printed by: York Publishing Services Ltd
64 Hallfield Road, Layerthorpe, York YO31 7ZQ

Tel: 01904 431213

Website: www.yps-publishing.co.uk

THE UNEXPURGATED ADVENTURES OF

SHERLOCK HOLMES

Books in the Series:

A BALLS-UP IN BOHEMIA
THE MYSTERIOUS CASE OF MR. GINGERNUTS
THE CASE OF THE RANDY STEPFATHER
MY FIRST PROPER RURAL MURDER
THE ORANGES OF DEATH!
THE MAN WITH THE HAIRY FACE
A GANDER AT THE BLUE CARBUNCLE
THE SPECKLED BAND SPECULATION
THE ADVENTURE OF THE ENGINEER'S TONGUE
THE MYSTERIOUS MARRIAGE OF THE GAY BACHELOR
THE SECRET PREDICAMENT OF THE STUPID BANKER
THE ADVENTURES OF THE PSYCHEDELIC TREES

Nicholas Sercombe is a writer and producer for film and television. He has been lucky enough to work in comedy for most of the Holocene period with some of the greatest performers and writers. He is most comfortable when reading Conan Doyle and even happier when re-writing these extraordinarily entertaining stories by Dr. John Watson.

Juliet Snape studied illustration at Cambridge School of Art and Central St. Martins. She has illustrated over 100 books and her work has been published around the world.

She is a fan of Sherlock Holmes – her father even lived in Baker Street – and, in the words of Conan Doyle, she is *"naturally gravitated to London, that great cesspool into which all the loungers and idlers of the Empire are irresistibly drained."* She lives in London and loves sketching, finding inspiration all around her. She has two children, both successful creatives.

For lovers of narcotics who indulge themselves like Sherlock Holmes – for fun and laughter.

The Adventures of the Psychedelic Trees

(published in The Strand in June 1892 with the title
THE ADVENTURE OF THE COPPER BEECHES
by Dr. Watson and Arthur Conan Doyle)

I had spent the night away from Baker Street on a jolly with fellow authors that contributed to *The Strand* magazine. It was a chilly September morning when I made my entrance into the apartment carrying the latest issue. I dropped it onto the most comfortable armchair of the two by the fireside with every intention of using it as soon as possible – it had been a very long night – and was surprised to find Sherlock Holmes out of bed and hard at work with his chemistry set.

'I say, Holmes, what have you got on the boil there?'

'To the man who loves art for its own sake,' remarked Sherlock Holmes, tossing aside the advertisement sheet of the *Daily Telegraph* that had just been used to mop up a small pool of what seemed to be hydrogen cyanide, reading the label of the bottle lying on its side adjacent, 'it is frequently in its least important and lowliest manifestations that the keenest pleasure is to be derived.'

My companion pointed to the laboratory apparatus he had constructed on the Napoleon escritoire, which he had moved across from the vestibule to one of the windows overlooking the street, no doubt to take in the activities of the passers-by whilst performing his dark arts. It was one of many of Holmes's assemblies that I had witnessed over the last couple of years, since I had moved into 221B Baker Street, and it was in full operation, boiling and bubbling and hissing like an angry locomotive.

'I don't know about lowly, Holmes. That is the biggest one yet.'

Proudly, he pointed to individual elements of the system. 'This experimental spider's web of laboratory glass is frontier chemistry, Watson, starting with these compounds immersed in those flasks which are being boiled up. The residue distils through this spiral of pipes here, through a condenser there and arrives in that beaker over there, right at the end. The resultant potion will be giving immense pleasure to the consumer, or consumers, dear Doctor.'

'And what is that "potion" going to be? Will it be a perfume? A strong spirit? Or your old friend, a narcotic?'

'A narcotic, Watson, of course, and one that has never been experienced before. For the moment I just call it my concoction. Something I am pleased to inform you is the result of many hours research and drawing up. There is a concentration of *Amanita Muscaria* here, an Algaric mushroom in the flask there. In that one there is the Peyotl cactus. There's a few of nature's other wonders dotted around in these flasks here, ideas that may help to produce something that is an hitherto unknown distraction. Now, we must wait and see what comes out and I shall write up the results into a treatise. Goodness me, I need a smoke of some fine tobacco! Where are my Sullivan Powell's?'

Holmes took a well-needed break and sampled some of the production line.

Holmes marched over to the fireplace. He took up a glowing cinder with the tongs and lit one of the oval No.2's. He drew in two lungs of the Burlington Arcade tobacconist's finest Turkish shag and exhaled slowly. He collected up the magazine I had dropped deliberately upon my arrival and plumped himself down in the same armchair, the one that I had bagged for myself. I took up residence opposite in the slightly less comfortable seat whilst he flicked through the contents. He landed upon the latest tale of our adventures together – the one about the banker stupid enough to take a valuable piece of jewellery home instead of leaving it in the bank – and flicked his eyes down the lines of text.*

'It is pleasant to me to observe, Watson,' mused he, 'that you have so far grasped this truth that in these little records of our cases which you have been good enough to draw up, and, I am bound to say, occasionally to embellish, you have given prominence not so much to the many *causes célèbres* and sensational trials in which I have figured, but rather those incidents which may have been trivial in themselves, but which have given room for those faculties of deduction and of logical synthesis which I have made my special province.'

'And yet,' said I, smiling, 'I cannot quite hold myself absolved from the charge of sensationalism which has been urged against my records. And I say that after that hound, George Newnes, has savagely edited each of my manuscripts prior to publication.'

'You have erred, perhaps,' he observed, 'in attempting to put colour and life into each of your statements, instead of confining yourself to the task of

* see *The Mysterious Marriage of the Gay Bachelor*

placing upon a record that severe reasoning from cause to effect, which is really the only notable feature about the thing.'

'It seems to me that I have done you full justice in the matter,' I remarked with some coldness, for I was repelled by the egotism which I had more than once observed to be a strong factor in my friend's singular character. 'The way I have portrayed you, your deductions are as certain as night follows day and your character is unimpeachable.'

'No, it is not selfishness or conceit,' said he, answering, as was his wont, my thoughts rather than my words. 'If I claim full justice for my art, it is because it is an impersonal thing – a thing beyond myself. Crime is common. Logic is rare. Therefore it is upon the logic rather than upon the crime that you should dwell. You have degraded what should have been a course of lectures into a series of tales.'

'It is what the public wants, Holmes!' cried I, leaning forward in my seat to make my point. 'I tell you, the proof is in the pudding! Sales of *The Strand* have increased exponentially since our adventures together have been revealed. And you are, now, somewhat a Society celebrity, as our trip to Ascot races proved.'*

'That, dear Doctor, I cannot make an argument against. At the same time,' he remarked, after a pause, during which he had sat puffing at his cigarette and gazing down at the fire, 'you can hardly be open to a charge of sensationalism, for out of these cases which you have been so kind as to interest yourself in, a fair proportion do not treat crime, in its legal sense, at all.

* see *The Adventure of The Engineer's Tongue*

The small matter in which I endeavoured to help the King of Bohemia, the singular experience of Miss Mary Sutherland, the problem connected with the man with the hairy face, and the incident of the gay bachelor, were all matters which are outside the pale of the law. But in avoiding the sensational, I fear that you have bordered on the trivial.'

Bloody cheek!

'The end may have been so,' I answered, 'but the methods I hold to have been novel and of interest.'

'Pshaw, my dear fellow! What do the public, the great unobservant public, who could hardly tell a weaver by his tooth or a compositor by his left thumb, care about the finer shades of analysis and deduction! But, indeed, if you are trivial, I cannot blame you, for the days of the great cases are past. Man, or at least criminal man, has lost all enterprise and originality. As to my own little practice, it seems to be degenerating into an agency for recovering lost pencils and giving advice to young ladies from boarding schools. I think that I have touched the bottom at last, however. This note which arrived this morning marks the lowest point, I fancy. Just take a look at it, Doctor!'

He tossed a crumpled letter across to me. It was dated from Montague Place upon the preceding evening, and ran thus:

'Dear Mr. Holmes – I am very anxious to consult you as to whether I should or should not accept a situation which has been offered to me as governess. I shall call at half-past ten tomorrow, if I do not inconvenience you. – Yours faithfully, Violet Hunter.

Do you know the young lady?' I asked.

'No, certainly not.'

'You are about to meet her. It is ten thirty and I am certain that is the ring of the doorbell now. Don't look so glum, my friend! This may turn out to be of more interest than you think. You remember that the affair of the blue carbuncle, which appeared to be a mere whim at first, developed into a serious investigation? It may be so in this case also.'*

'Well, let us hope so! My doubts will very soon be solved, for here, unless I am much mistaken, is the person in question.'

As he spoke the door opened. Mrs. Hudson entered the room with a young lady in her wake. Holmes and I stood up.

'Mr. Holmes, a Miss Hunter is here to see you. Blimey! There's a hell of a fug in here!'

'Mrs. Hudson, there is bound to be a fug,' said Holmes. Then, he tried to be a comedian. 'It is Watson – he has been out on the tiles all night. Please, bring refreshments for our guest.'

Our landlady stared at the apparatus, glared at Sherlock Holmes, huffed and puffed, tutted to herself, muttered something about "burning the place down, if you are not too careful" and exited. We turned our eyes upon our guest, who stood patiently but with notable confidence, her nose twitching purposefully to gauge the thickness of the air. She was plainly but neatly dressed, with a bright, quick face, freckled like a plover's egg, but there was nothing demure about Miss Hunter. She had the brisk manner of a woman who has had her own way to make in the world.

* see *A Gander at the Blue Carbuncle*

'You will excuse my troubling you, I am sure,' said she in an unselfconscious voice, as my companion rose and walked over to greet her, 'but I have had a very strange experience. I have no parents or relations of any sort from whom I might ask advice. I have been told that you are a man of the world, Mr. Holmes. I thought that perhaps you would be kind enough to advise me what I should do.'

'Good morning, Miss Hunter,' gushed the great detective, whilst taking her hand in both of his and smothering her with his gaze. I could see by the appreciative smile on his face that he was favourably impressed by the assertive manner and commanding speech of his new client. Oh goodness no, he fancied her!

'Pray, take my seat. I shall be happy to do anything that I can to serve you. Move out of the way, Watson!'

Whilst my companion had vacated the comfortable chair, I had taken my chance to slip into it myself. However, I was obliged to stand up again and greet Miss Hunter, who shook my hand whilst looking me in the eye. As soon as I rose from the seat, Holmes lowered her gracefully into it. Just as I was on a downward trajectory to park my arse back where I started, I felt strong, hairy hands grab my shoulders and lift me forcibly to one side.

'Thank you, Watson, I am consulting...'

My companion swiftly parked himself in my seat and drew it forward, so he may be closer to Miss Hunter. 'Please, Miss, tell me about your circumstances and I shall try to act *in loco parentis* to the best of my ability.'

And as the great detective studied Miss Hunter's complexion in detail, I searched for the nearest spare seat. I dragged a dining chair into an adjacent position and lumped myself down upon it with a sigh of resignation and tiredness. You should have seen how Holmes had composed himself! He had rested his elbows upon the arms of the chair, pressed his finger-tips together and parked his chin upon them. His lids were all droopy and he had a stupid, bemused look upon his face, like a puppy with colic. He was infatuated.

'Please, Miss Hunter, begin your story.'

'I have been a governess for five years,' said she, authoritatively, 'in the family of Colonel Matt Munro, but two months ago the Colonel received an appointment at Halifax, in Nova Scotia, and took his children over to America with him, so I found myself without a situation. I advertised and I answered advertisements, but without success. At last the little money which I had saved began to run short, and I was at my wits' end as to what I should do.'

'There is a well-known agency for governesses in the West End called Westaway's and there I used to call about once a week in order to see whether anything had turned up which might suit me. Westaway was the name of the founder of the business, but it is really managed by Miss Stoper. She sits in her own little office, and the ladies who are seeking employment wait in an ante-room, and are then shown in one by one, when she consults her ledgers, and sees whether she has anything which would suit them.'

'Well, when I was called last week I was shown the little office as usual, but I found that Miss Stoper was not alone. A prodigiously stout man with a very smiling face, and a great heavy chin which rolled down in fold upon fold over his throat, sat at her elbow with a pair of glasses on his nose, looking very earnestly at the ladies who entered. As I came in he gave quite a jump in his chair and turned quickly to Miss Stoper.'

'"That will do," said he; "I could not ask for anything better. Capital! Capital!"' He seemed quite enthusiastic and rubbed his hands together in the most genial fashion. He was such a comfortable-looking man that it was quite a pleasure to look at him.

'"You are looking for a situation, Miss?"'

'"Yes, sir."'

'"As governess?"'

'"Yes, sir"'

'"And what salary do you ask?"'

'"I had four pounds a month in my last place with Colonel Munro."'

'"Matt Munro? Oh, tut, tut! Sweating! Rank sweating!" he cried, throwing his fat hands out into the air like a man who is in a boiling passion. "I adore his voice, Miss Hunter! But how could anyone offer so pitiful a sum to a lady with such attractions and accomplishments?"'

'"My accomplishments, sir, are practical but maybe less than you imagine," said I. "I have a little French. *Ein bissen* off ze German! I have an ear for music; the pianoforte and church organ are at my beck and call. And as for drawing! Well, let me tell you…"'

'"That's enough, Miss Hunter!" he cried. "This is all quite beside the question. The point is, have you or have you not the bearing and deportment of a lady? There it is in a nutshell. If you have not, you are not fitted for the rearing of a child who may someday play a considerable part in the history of the country. But if you have, then how could any gentleman ask you to condescend to accept anything under the three figures? Your salary with me, madam, would commence at a hundred pounds a year"'

'You may imagine, Mr. Holmes, that to me, destitute as I was, such an offer seemed almost too good to be true. The gentleman, however, seeing perhaps the look of incredulity upon my face, opened a pocket-book and took out a note.'

'"It is my custom," said he, smiling in the most pleasant fashion until his eyes were just two shining slits, amid the white creases of his face, "to advance my young ladies half their salary beforehand, so that they may meet any little expenses of their journey and their wardrobe."'

'It seemed to me that I had never met so fascinating and so thoughtful a man. As I was already in debt to my tradesmen, the advance was a great convenience, and yet there was something unnatural about the whole transaction which made me wish to know a little more before I quite committed myself.'

'"May I ask you where you live, sir?"'

'"Hampshire. Charming rural place. The Copper Beeches, which is five miles on the far side of Winchester. It is the loveliest country, my dear young lady, and the dearest old country house."'

'"And my duties, sir? I should be glad to know what they would be."'

'"One child – one dear little romper, just six years old. Oh, if you could see him killing cockroaches with a slipper! Smack! Smack, smack, smack! Four gone before you could wink!" He leaned back in his chair and laughed his eyes into his head again.'

Holmes flicked a mischievous glance at me. I played bluff innocent from my rather uncomfortable chair.

'I was a little startled at the nature of the child's amusement,' she continued, most sternly, 'but the father's laughter made me think that perhaps he was joking.'

'"My sole duties, then," I asked, "are to take charge of a single child?"'

'"No, no, not the sole, not the sole, my dear young lady," he cried. "Your duty would be, as I am sure your good sense would suggest, to obey any little commands which my wife may give, provided always that they were such commands as a lady might with propriety obey. You see no difficulty, heh?"'

'"I should be happy to make myself useful."'

'"Quite so. In dress now, for example! We are faddy people, you know…"'

'What on Earth is faddy?' I enquired.

'Shut up, Watson! Ignore him, Miss Hunter.'

But she did quite the opposite. Miss Hunter turned to face me. Her eyes bored into mine and she pointed at my nose.

'Faddy, Doctor Watson, turns out to mean strange, weird, unusual, uncanny, peculiar and, I don't know, wonderful? All rolled into one. It turns out that this fat-chinned wonder of Miss Stoper's wanted me to: "wear any dress which we might give you" and then he suggested it was: "our little whim." Whim! I would call him and his wife debauched. However, money talks, gentlemen, so I agreed to go along with the proposal. But then, he went further. He said:

'"My wife and I may wish to choose for you where you sit. It may be here. It may be there. Would that be offensive?"'

'"Er, no, I suppose not..."' I answered. But then he blotted his copybook beyond my tolerances, Mr. Holmes, Doctor Watson. Then, he told me this:

'"We would insist on you cutting your hair quite short before you come to us."'

'I could hardly believe my ears! As you may observe, Mr. Holmes, my hair is somewhat luxuriant, and of a rather peculiar tint of chestnut.'

'Oh, it is very much luxuriant!' gushed the great detective, on heat. 'I would call your hair artistic.'

'Precisely correct, Mr. Holmes! I could not dream of sacrificing it. So, I told him exactly that. "I am afraid that is quite impossible," I said, and I could see a shadow pass over his face as I spoke.'

'You were losing his interest?'

'Yes, Doctor, I had. He said that short hair "is a little fancy of my wife's" and it is "essential."'

'So, she is the true pervert of the pair?'

'Shut up, Watson!' stamped Holmes.

'He asked me again: "You won't cut your hair?"'

'"No, sir, I really could not," I answered firmly.'

'"Ah, very well, then that quite settles the matter. It is a pity, because in other respects you would have done very nicely. In that case, Miss Stoper, I had best inspect a few more of your young ladies."'

I couldn't help thinking to myself that this whole concept of lining up young ladies and letting a chap make a little conversation and then make his choice for the duration was mighty close to last night's final resting place for the authors of *The Strand*. This was a very clean and tidy house in South Kensington, not far from Queensbury Place, where my surgery used to be. This establishment had a certain style of its own in which the assuming madame who owned it, herself a very perceptive lady, would interview her "guests" most intimately and, after a while, would make up her mind as to which bedroom she would send said "guest." Each room had a young lady in residence who would be the closest match for her client's short-term happiness. Naturally, the madame's reputation was staked upon her judgment of character. Did it work? Well, her house was full to the brim every night and the name Lady Bonking was a byword for top pimping in the civilised world. Famously, though, there is a very amusing story about Lady Bonking's unique matching service which once went awry that is whispered by roisterers and the rollickers around town. It is about an evening during the war when she interviewed a new guest: a young guardsman who was in dire need of womanly companionship. Lady B made her assessment and directed him to the chosen bedroom. When the young blade arrived, it was his sister who answered the door!

'Pay attention, Doctor!'

'My apologies, Holmes, but I was... I say!' I suddenly realised that it was not Sherlock Holmes who had reprimanded me but our guest! She stared at me, no hint of a blink. I moved my position until I was erect. She nodded approval.

'Pray, Miss Hunter,' said the great detective, 'tell us what became of you after your decision to decline the offer of the position. And sit up straight, Watson!'

Ha, ha, bloody ha...

'Well, Mr. Holmes, the manageress had sat all the while busy with her papers without saying a word. She glanced at me now with so much annoyance upon her face that I could not help suspecting that she had lost a handsome commission through my refusal. She asked me whether I wished to remain on her books and when I said that I would she was most terse in her reply. She said that I could hardly expect her to find openings for me that I would not accept. She struck a tinker bell upon the table and I was shown out by the page boy.'

'When I arrived back at my lodgings and looked inside the empty cupboards and bare shelves of the larder I began to ask myself whether I had not done a very foolish thing. After all, if these people had strange fads, and expected obedience on the most extraordinary matters, they were at least ready to pay for their eccentricity. Very few governesses in England are getting a hundred a year. Besides, what use was my hair to me? Many people are improved by wearing it short.'

'Certainly, that is the case for Doctor Watson there!' quipped Sherlock Holmes, and we all laughed politely at his pathetic attempt to ease Miss Hunter's knickers down.

'Next day I was inclined to think that I had made a mistake, and by the day after I was sure of it. I had almost overcome my pride, so far as to go back to the agency and inquire whether the place was still open, when I received this letter from the gentleman himself. I have it here. I shall read it to you:

'Dear Miss Hunter – Miss Stoper has very kindly given me your address, and I write from my beautiful country house near Winchester to ask you whether you have reconsidered your decision. My wife is very anxious that you should come. We are willing to give thirty pounds a quarter, or £120 a year, so as to recompense you for any little inconvenience which our fads may cause you. They are not very exacting after all. My wife is fond of a particular shade of electric blue and would like you to wear such a dress indoors in the morning. You need not, however, go to the expense of purchasing one, as we have one belonging to my dear daughter Alice (now in Philadelphia) which would, I think, fit you very well. Then, as to sitting in certain spots that we may choose for you, that need cause you no inconvenience. As regards your hair, it may be beautiful in its present style, but we insist upon it being cut short. It will grow again, and I hope that the increased salary may recompense you for the temporary loss. Now do try to come, and I shall meet you with a dog-cart at Winchester. Let me know your train. Yours faithfully, Jethro Rucastle.'

'That is the letter which I have just received, Mr. Holmes, and my mind is made up that I will accept. I thought, however, that before taking the final step, I should like to submit the whole matter to you.'

'Well, Miss Hunter, if your mind is made up, that settles the question,' said Holmes, smiling. 'I suspect you have come here for an additional reason. My alter-ego is delighted to offer my services to you.'

'For what, Mr. Holmes?' she enquired, somewhat piqued.

'As the Golden Scissors, of course!'

'To whom do you refer? *What* do you refer to?'

'The Golden Scissors of Soho, Miss Hunter,' announced I proudly. 'You are in the most fortunate position of consulting him right now.'

'As if you didn't know!' chided the great hairdresser, looking all modest. 'It will be my absolute pleasure to service you.'

'To do *what* to me, Mr. Holmes?!' she cried.

I could see there was a desolation of misunderstanding. I stood up. 'Why, to cut and style your luxuriant hair, Miss Hunter. Mr. Sherlock Holmes is none other than The Golden Scissors of Soho!'

'Oh, I had no idea. Right, well, I... Thank goodness!'

Sherlock Holmes sprang to his feet and marched off to the Sheraton tallboy from which he extracted his Gladstone bag, the one in which he stashed his fine instruments of the coif.*

'What do you make of it all, Mr. Holmes?' asked our new client. 'What is the meaning?'

'I have no data. I cannot tell,' said Holmes, now moving in behind Miss Hunter in the comfy chair. He opened his bag. 'Perhaps the good Doctor has formed an opinion of the medical variety?'

'Well, I am glad that you have asked me. To me there can only be one solution. Mr. Rucastle seems to be a very kind, good-natured man who has realised that his wife is a lesbian.'

Miss Hunter clapped her hand to her mouth and emitted a muffled squeak. Holmes raised his brows.

'Instead of letting her go,' I continued, 'he has desires to keep the matter quiet for fear she should take

* see *The Man with the Hairy Face*

off and leave him. Therefore, he humours her fancies in every way in order to prevent a walk-out.'

'That is a possible solution, Watson, but maybe not a probable one. *Les-be* having a think about it!'

'Oh, very dry, Holmes!'

'But might his wife be just an eccentric?'

'No. All the indicators of lesbianism are there. The specific clothing. The seating positions. The short hair. But, moreover, it was the reaction of Mr. Rucastle to his first sighting of Miss Hunter. Obviously, he is aware of his wife's sensual preferences. Miss Hunter's features are so close to his wife's *bella giovane ninfa* that he offered an immense salary to induce her acceptance without question. Furthermore, the fact that he has increased the offer demonstrates he has reported back to his wife, described Miss Hunter's features, and her desires have overwhelmed them both.'

'Thank you, Watson. That is remarkably incisive.'

Holmes walked round to face Miss Hunter. 'So, Miss Hunter, you came to me to ask my advice. My opinion is that the Rucastles offer may be generous but it does not seem to be a very nice household for a young lady to live in.'

'But the money, Mr. Holmes, the money!'

'Well, yes, of course, the pay is good – too good. That is what makes me uneasy. Why should they give you £120 a year to look after one child when they could pay you £40? There must be another, strong reason behind.'

'There is danger,' I added. 'A danger that Mrs. Rucastle will make advances upon you of the soft-shoe variety, Miss Hunter.'

'Yes, I would say it is a distinct danger,' said Holmes, solemnly, 'that Mrs. Rucastle favours ladies.'

'Well, I have made a decision!' cried our client, standing up straight to emphasise her judgment. 'I shall go down to Hampshire and take the position. I shall write to Mr. Rucastle at once and you may, if you will, Mr. Holmes, make a start on my poor hair.'

Holmes brightened at once. 'It will be my greatest pleasure,' said he, capering back into position behind Miss Hunter. 'Please, sit down again.'

Holmes started to stroke her beautiful chestnut-coloured hair over and over. 'It is a rare day now when I am allowed the artistic freedom to coif such elegant locks, or, that I may expose such a ravishingly-exquisite neck as yours.'

And to my great surprise, and I swear, dear reader, that The Golden Scissors of Soho leaned forward and planted a kiss upon her equally ravishingly-exquisite nape!

* * *

A fortnight went by, during which I frequently found my thoughts turning in her direction, and I was wondering what strange side-alley of human experience this lonely woman had strayed into. The unusual salary, the curious conditions, the light duties, all pointed towards something abnormal, though whether a fad or a plot, or whether the man were a philanthropist or a villain, it was quite beyond my powers to determine. As to Holmes, I observed that he sat frequently for half an hour on end, with knitted brows and an abstracted air, but he swept the matter away with a wave of his hand when I mentioned it. 'Data! Data! Data!' he cried impatiently. 'I can't make bricks without clay.' And yet he would always wind-up muttering that no sister of his would ever have accepted such a situation. Too right! Rachel was much too intelligent to have her mind tied to raising other peoples' children. However, I knew that Holmes had become infatuated by Miss Violet Hunter, the first woman to grab his attention since Irene Adler. And when he had finished the *coup savage* on her long, luxuriant hair her beauty beamed out like an Argand lamp shining forth from the tallest lighthouse. The Golden Scissors had created a style known as "The Robert." She was an attractive lady, albeit in a very strict, school-marmy way, but this is what Sherlock Holmes found so alluring in her.

The telegram came late one night, just as I was thinking of turning in, and Holmes was settling down to one of those all-night activities which he frequently indulged in; this time he was decanting the result of the experiment that I had found him with a couple of weeks ago. He had dried out the resultant liquid over a period of days. Now, he had been left an off-white powder which he was making into tablets using a small compressor. I hoped not to find him in the same position when I came down to breakfast in the morning. He opened the yellow envelope, and then, glancing at the message, threw it across to me.

'Just look up the trains in Bradshaw,' said he, and turned back to his chemical studies.

The summons was a brief and urgent one:

'Dear Mr. Holmes – please be at the Black Swan Hotel at Winchester at midday tomorrow,' it said. *'Do come! I am at my wits end. Yours, Violet Hunter'*

I recognised Holmes's foreplay and dreaded what was coming next!

‘Will you come?’ asked Holmes, looking up at me.

‘I am the official chronicler. Just try and stop me, old friend!’

‘Just look up the train times, then.’

‘There is a train at half-past nine,’ said I, glancing over my Bradshaw. ‘It is due at Winchester at 11.30.’

‘That will do very nicely. Then perhaps I had better finish my pill production, as we may need to be at our best in the morning.’

I agreed with him. He scooped up the loose white tablets and channelled them into an amber glass medicine bottle.

‘By the way, Watson – bring your revolver tomorrow. I have a funny feeling…’

‘If you say so, Holmes.’

I think he wanted to impress Miss Hunter with the Manstopper, but I didn’t say anything. We turned in early for the night.

* * *

We arrived at Waterloo station in good order the next morning. Holmes checked that I had remembered to bring the Manstopper, which I brought out of its new shoulder holster with a flourish (for I had been practising my quick-draw) and showed it to him on the concourse, much to the distress of some neighbouring fellow travellers. He, with respect to my flourish, whipped out the medicine bottle of pills that he had compressed the night before and rattled them around. I didn’t enquire why he had brought them – I just rolled my eyes in despair.

By eleven o'clock we were well upon our way to the old English capital. Holmes had been buried in the morning papers all the way down, but after we had passed the Hampshire border he threw them down and began to admire the scenery. It was an ideal day, a light blue sky, flecked with little fleecy white clouds drifting across from west to east. The sun was shining very brightly, and yet there was an exhilarating nip in the air, which set an edge to a man's energy. All over the countryside, away to the rolling hills around Aldershot, and then onto the market town of Basingstoke, the little red and grey roofs of the farm-steadings peeped out from amidst the green of the foliage.

'I say, Holmes. Isn't this beautiful?' I cried, with all the enthusiasm of a man fresh from the fug of Baker Street.

But Holmes shook his head gravely.

'Do you know, Watson,' said he, 'that it is one of the worst curses of the mind with a turn like mine that I must look at everything with reference to my own special subject. You look at these scattered houses, and you are impressed by their beauty. I look at them, and the only thought which comes to me is a feeling of their isolation, and of the impunity with which crime may be committed there.'

'Good heavens!' who would associate crime with these dear old homesteads?'

'They always fill me with a certain horror. It is my belief, Watson, founded upon my experience, that the lowest and vilest alleys in London do not present a more dreadful record of sin than does the smiling and beautiful countryside.'

'What a lot of rot, Holmes! You have a gloomy speculation. What do you imagine scenes of? Be-whiskered yokels chasing young virgins around the fields? Dirty old cider-riddled farmers lurking naked in the woodsheds? Women's sewing circles plotting gory, midsomer murders? Parish council meetings a hotbed for wife swopping child abusers? No, Holmes, they are not! The reality is much more simple -- you are a paranoid townie!'

'Certainly not. My theory has substance. The pressure of public opinion can do in the town what the law cannot accomplish. There is no lane so vile that the scream of a tortured child, or the thud of a drunkard's blow, does not beget sympathy and indignation among the neighbours, and the whole machinery of justice is ever so close that a word of complaint can set it going, and there is but a step between the crime and the dock. Just look at these lonely houses, each in its own fields, filled for the most part with poor ignorant folk who know little of the law. Think of the deeds of hellish cruelty, the hidden wickedness which may go on, year in, year out, in such places, and no one is the wiser.'

'But Holmes, the problem with your theory is that the country folk are decent, Christian people. They don't need to be aware of the laws that punish the crimes you speak about. The trouble with cities is that they attract the detritus of humanity as well as the luminaries.'

'Hmm! Take, for instance, Miss Hunter,' mused the master detective. 'Had this lady who appeals to us for help gone to live in Winchester, I should never have had a fear for her. It is the five miles of country which makes the danger. Still, it is clear that she is not personally threatened.'

'No, if she can come to Winchester to meet us she can get away.'

'Quite so. She has her freedom.'

'What *can* be the matter, then? What on Earth are we doing on this train? Ah, but I think we know, don't we? Miss Hunter has distracted your eye!'

'Oh don't be ridiculous!'

'Just take a look at yourself. You could not have been more sceptical about her first entreaty to you. But as soon as she gave you that smouldering-stern interview, you took the bait. When you cut her hair into a Robert, the intimacy overcame you. Lust was washing over you, desire coursing through your veins...'

'Shut up, Watson!'

'Ah, you cannot stand it! Having your mind diverted by anything in this life is an upset for the great Sherlock Holmes. But a woman? A woman! No, there lies a terrible weakness in the great detective's resolve, which is NOT allowed.'

'I have devised seven separate explanations, each of which would cover the facts as far as we know them. But which of these is correct can only be determined by the fresh information which we shall no doubt find waiting for us?'

'Well, look over there, Holmes. That is the tower of the cathedral. We shall soon learn all that Miss Hunter has to tell. However, my bet is that Mrs. Rucastle has made an invitation to Miss Hunter of the kipper-licking kind.'

'Watson, your army lexicon is as colourful as ever, but I have to admit that it is one of the seven. Come, let us get our things down and get ready to disembark. The game's afoot!'

* * *

The Black Swan is an inn of repute in the High Street, at no distance from the railway station, and there we found the young lady waiting for us. She had engaged a sitting-room, and our cold crab and lobster lunch awaited us upon the table.

'Well done. You made it,' said she with the authority of a Sergeant Major. 'It is so kind of you both; but indeed I am not sure quite what I should do. Your advice will be altogether invaluable to me.'

'Pray, tell us what has happened to you?'

'I will do so. Now, sit down. I shall be quick for I have promised Mr. Rucastle to be back before three o'clock. I got his leave to come into town this morning, but I did not give him a reason. Doctor, please pour the Mersault.'

I was surprised by the change in her manner. When she consulted Sherlock Holmes in the first place she had a voice of authority but now she was a stern dictator.

'Let us have everything in its due order.' Holmes tucked his long thin legs under the table and composed himself to listen.

'In the first place, I may say that I have met, on the whole, with no actual ill-treatment from Mr. and Mrs. Rucastle.'

'Well, then, I'll be off!' said I, rising up from my seat and chortling inside at my comedic routine. But there was an awkward laguna, not even a smile from Holmes or Miss Hunter or, indeed, any other living being in the Black Swan inn. My joke was a train crash, with massive loss of life. I sat back down.

'Miss Hunter, please excuse his simply dreadful sense of humour.'

'This is seriously unamusing, Doctor,' she muttered seriously. 'Sit down and have your lunch.'

How about that for a put-down? We started to eat and I was trying my very best to avoid my companion's Cheshire-cat smile but failing miserably. He just couldn't stop himself from grinning.

'Anyway, Mr. Holmes, even though the Rucastles have behaved themselves thus far, I cannot understand them. I am not easy in my mind about them.'

'What can you not understand?' cooed the great detective.

'The reasons for their conduct. But you shall have it all just as it occurred. When I came down Mr. Rucastle met me here and drove me in his dog-cart to his house, Copper Beeches. It is, as he said, beautifully situated, but it is not beautiful in itself, for it is a large square block of a house, whitewashed, but all stained and streaked with damp and bad weather. There are grounds round it – woods on three sides, and on the fourth a field which slopes down to the Southampton high-road, which curves past, about a hundred yards from the front door. This ground in front belongs to the house, but the woods all round are part of Lord Southerton's preserves. A clump of copper beeches immediately in front of the hall door has given its name to the place.'

'I was driven there by my new employer, who was as amiable as ever, and was introduced by him that evening to his wife and the child. There was no truth, Mr. Holmes, in the conjecture which seemed to us to be probable in your rooms at Baker Street. Mrs. Rucastle is not mad.'

Holmes and I raised brows at each other.

'I found her to be a silent, pale-faced woman, much younger than her husband, not more than thirty, I should think, while he can hardly be less than forty-five. From their conversation I have gathered that they have been married about seven years, that he was a widower, and that his only child by his first wife was the daughter who has gone to Philadelphia. Mr. Rucastle told me in private that the reason why she had left them was that she had an unreasoning aversion to her stepmother...'

Our brows rose up another notch as our memories harmonised upon my theorem of earlier. Had the daughter discovered that her new mother was a lesbian?

'As the daughter could not have been less than twenty, I can quite imagine that her position must have been uncomfortable with her father's young wife.'

'Quite. But what is she like, Miss Hunter?'

'She is a nonentity. She seems to be passionately devoted to her husband and to her little son. During our first encounter her light grey eyes wandered continually from one to the other. He was kind to her also in his bluff, boisterous fashion, and on the whole they seemed to be a happy couple. And yet she had something secret hidden away because since our introduction I would find her alone, lost in deep thought. More than once I have surprised her in tears. I have thought sometimes that it is the disposition of her child which weighed heavily upon her mind, for I have never met so utterly spoilt and so ill-natured a little creature. He is small for his age, with a head which is quite disproportionately large. His whole life appears to be spent in an alternation between savage fits of passion and gloomy intervals of sulking. Giving pain to any creature weaker than himself seems to be his one idea of amusement, and he shows quite a remarkable talent in planning the capture of mice, little birds, and insects. But I would rather not talk about the creature, Mr. Holmes, and, indeed, he has little to do with my story.'

'I am glad of all details,' remarked my friend, 'even if this child is a brat, we can help you to take care of it. Watson! You remembered to bring that special item I requested before we turned in last night?'

'I did, Holmes, I have it here.' I stroked the huge lump on the left side of my coat where the Henry Holland 0.577 Manstopper resided.

'I shall try not to miss anything of importance. The one unpleasant thing about the house, which struck me at once, was the appearance and conduct of the servants. There are only two: a man and his wife. Toller, for this is his name, is a rough, uncouth man, with grizzled hair and whiskers, and a perpetual smell of drink. Twice since I have been with them he has been quite drunk, and yet, Mr. Rucastle seemed to take no notice of it. Fluffy, for that is her name, his wife, is a very tall and strong woman with a sour face, as silent as Mrs. Rucastle, and much less amiable. They are a most unpleasant couple, but fortunately I spend most

Personally, I would use split bamboo on children …
"Spare the rod and spoil the child,"
quad erat demonstrandum!

of my time in the nursery and my own room, which are next to each other in one corner of the building.'

'For two days after my arrival at the Copper Beeches my life was very quiet; on the third, Mrs. Rucastle came down after breakfast and whispered something to her husband. Mr. Rucastle looked over to me.

'"We are very much obliged to you, Miss Hunter, for falling in with our whims so far as to cut your hair. I assure you that it has not detracted the tiniest iota from your appearance. In fact, Mrs. Rucastle remarked to me in bed last night how pretty your face sits in that small, neat nest of beautifully shiny hair. We shall now see how the electric blue dress will become you. You will find it laid out upon the bed in your room, and if you would be so good as to put it on we should both be extremely obliged."'

It was at this point that Miss Hunter placed her knife and fork neatly together upon her plate. She stood up, patted her napkin on her lips and made her excuses.

'Off for a wee,' said I, watching our client swinging her hips nicely as she headed off to find a convenience. 'She has a stern way with her words, what?'

'She is a governess, Watson. If you misbehave, like you did just now, do not expect to be treated with kid gloves; expect to be treated like a miscreant child.' Holmes leaned back in his seat and lit up a Sobranie sub-rosa. 'I can tell you – I find her manner most attractive.'

We sat in contemplative silence a while. I was still peckish and yearned for something in the pudding department.

'Shall I ask to see the sweet trolley?'

'Only if you want to get us thrown out on the street. Hark! I hear our disciplinarian client returning. Let us find out all of the facts and see what we must do next before upsetting the yokels, Watson.'

Miss Hunter returned to the table and planted her peachy upon the seat.

'I shall continue,' she said, making herself comfortable and inclining her head towards me and then the bottle of wine. 'The dress which I found waiting for me was a peculiar shade of blue,' said she, as I poured the rather palatable Mersault. 'It was of excellent material – the softest cotton – but it bore unmistakable signs of having been worn before. It could not have been a better fit if I had been measured for it. Both Mr. and Mrs. Rucastle expressed a delight at the look of it which seemed quite exaggerated in its vehemence. They were waiting for me in the drawing-room, which is a very large room, stretching along the entire front of the house, with three long windows reaching down to the floor. A chair had been placed close to the central window, with its back turned towards it. In this I was asked to sit, and then Mr. Rucastle, walking up and down on the other side of the room, began to tell me a series of the funniest stories that I have ever listened to.'

Well, I thought to myself, he is called Jethro, and who would have imagined he was a master comedian with a name like that? But I didn't wish to say this out loud – the last time I made a jolly quip I was stamped on!

'You cannot imagine how comical he was, and I laughed until I was quite weary. Mrs. Rucastle, who has evidently no sense of humour, never so much as smiled, but sat with her hands in her lap, and a sad, anxious look upon her face, and, generally, staring at me. After an hour or so, Mr. Rucastle suddenly remarked that it was time to commence the duties of the day, and that I might change my dress, and go to Edward, the little tyke that he is.'

'Two days later this same performance was gone through under exactly similar circumstances. Again, I changed my dress. Again, I sat in the window and again I laughed heartily at the funny stories of which my employer had an immense repertoire, and which he told inimitably. Then he handed me a yellow-backed novel, and, moving my chair a little sideways, that my own shadow might not fall upon the page, he begged me to read aloud to him. I read for about ten minutes, beginning in the heart of a chapter, and then suddenly, in the middle of a sentence, he ordered me to cease and change my dress.

'You can easily imagine, Mr. Holmes, how curious I became as to what the meaning of this extraordinary performance could possibly be. They were always very careful, I observed, to turn my face away from the window, so that I became consumed with the desire to see what was going on behind my back. At first it seemed impossible, but soon I devised a means. My hand mirror had been broken, so a happy thought seized me, and I concealed a little of the glass in my handkerchief. On the next occasion, in the midst of my laughter, I put my handkerchief up to my eyes, and was able with a little manoeuvring to see all that was behind me. I confess that I was disappointed. There was nothing.'

'Really? You surprise me,' remarked the great detective.

'Don't interrupt, Mr. Holmes!' she exclaimed, with a cross brow and a little stamp of her right foot. 'I haven't finished my story yet!'

My companion was taken aback but then he smiled and wriggled back into his seat. Now, I could be absolutely certain that he found her most stimulating.

'When I took a second glance,' said she, purposefully, 'I perceived that there was a man standing in the Southampton road, a small bearded man in a grey suit, who seemed to be looking in my direction. The road is an important highway, and there are usually people there. This man, however, was leaning against the railings which bordered our field, and was looking earnestly. I lowered my handkerchief and glanced at Mrs. Rucastle to find her eyes fixed upon me with a most searching gaze. She said nothing, but I am convinced that she had divined that I had a mirror in my hand and had seen what was behind me. She rose at once.

'"Jethro!" she said. "There is an impertinent fellow upon the road there who stares up at Miss Hunter."'

'"A friend of yours, Miss Hunter?" he asked.'

'"No. I know of no one in these parts."'

'"Dear me! How very rude! Kindly turn around, and motion him to go away."'

'"Surely it would be better to take no notice?"'

'"No, we should have him loitering here always. Kindly turn around and wave him away like that."'

'I did as I was told, and at the same instant Mrs. Rucastle drew down the blind. That was a week ago, and from that time I have not sat again in the window, nor have I worn the blue dress, nor seen the man in the road.'

'Well, Miss Hunter, thank you. That is a fascinating story,' said Holmes.

'I haven't finished yet,' she said, tersely, but her eyes widened at me. 'You! Sit up straight!'

'Yes, Watson, stop slouching!'

He just couldn't resist, could he? But even so, I found myself making an effort to straighten my spine and lift my head up.

'Your narrative promises to be a most interesting one, Miss Hunter. My apologies for interrupting you.'

'You may find the rest of my story rather disconnected. I cannot perceive the relation between the different incidents of which I am about to speak. On the very first day that I was at Copper Beeches, Mr. Rucastle took me to a small outhouse which stands near the kitchen door. As we approached it I heard the sharp rattling of a chain, and the sounds of a large animal moving about.'

'"Look in here!" said Mr. Rucastle, showing me the slit between two planks. "Is he not a beauty?"'

'I looked through, half expecting to see a relation of his, but I could only see two glowing eyes, and a vague figure huddled up in the darkness.'

'"Don't be frightened," said my employer, laughing at the start which I had given. "It's only Carlo, my mastiff. I call him mine, but really old Toller, my groom, is the only man who can do anything with him. We feed him once a day, and not too much then, so that he is always as keen as mustard. Toller lets him loose every night, and God help the trespasser whom he lays his fangs upon. For goodness' sake, don't ever on any pretext set your foot over the threshold at night, for it is as much as your life is worth."'

'The warning was no idle one, for two nights later I happened to look out of my bedroom window about two o'clock in the morning. It was a beautiful moonlight night, and the lawn in front of the house was silvered over and almost as bright as day. I was standing wrapt by the peaceful beauty of the scene, when I was aware that something was moving under the shadow of the copper beeches. As it emerged into the moonshine I saw that it was a giant dog, as large as a calf, tawny-tinted, with hanging jowl, black muzzle, and huge projecting bones. It walked slowly across the lawn and vanished into the shadow upon the other side. That dreadful silent sentinel sent a chill to my heart.'

She sounded as if her story was complete. However, when I glanced at my companion, it was obvious that neither of us dare say a thing, or even move a muscle, for fear of being rebuked. We waited patiently, which was just as well...

'And now I have a *very* strange experience to tell you,' said our client, now leaning forwards to ensure we hung upon her every word 'You cut off my hair in London, Mr. Holmes, and I had placed it in a great coil at the bottom of my trunk. One evening, after the child was in bed, I began to amuse myself by examining the furniture in my room, and by rearranging my own little things. There was an old chest of drawers in the room, the two upper ones empty and open, the lower one locked. I had filled the two first with my linen, and as I had still much to pack away, I was naturally annoyed at not having use of the third drawer. I took out my bunch of keys and tried to open it. The very first key fitted to perfection. You will never guess what was inside!'

‘Inside was a coil of hair,’ remarked Holmes.

‘Absolutely correct! You are good.’

‘It was the same peculiar tint as yours and the same thickness.’

‘Correct again. On first sight I thought it may have been my own…’

‘But it was not. Yours was still in the trunk.’

‘But they were identical. Was it not extraordinary? I put theirs back in the drawer as I had found it and locked it up again. I said nothing of the matter to the Rucastles.’

‘Well, it is a strange coincidence, Miss Hunter,’ said Holmes, adjusting the weight of his seated posterior as if he may be about to stand, ‘and although your story is weirdly wonderful, I can see no reason to…’

‘I told you… I HAVEN’T FINISHED YET!’ cried our host, petulantly, like Torquemada after he’d mislaid the thumbscrews.

‘I’ll get another bottle,’ said I, and scooted out of my chair pronto on an escape mission to the bar. Whilst I was on the move, I could hear the great detective grovelling his humble apologies. On my return journey to the table, he was still talking and he was well into the final furlong of unnecessary explanation and, true to form, who was he blaming?

‘Anyway,’ said he, ‘it is the stress of him being an army doctor... Ah, Watson!’

‘Ah! Doctor Watson, thank you!’ said she, giving me one hell of look of sympathy and a supercilious smile. I poured the wine.

'Anyway, Mr. Holmes, back to my saga,' continued she. 'I had noticed that there was one wing of the house which appeared not to be inhabited at all. A door which faced that which led into the quarters of the Tollers opened into this suite, but it was invariably locked. One day, however, as I ascended the stair, I met Mr. Rucastle coming out through this door, his keys in his hand, and a look on his face which made him a very different person to the round, jovial man to whom I was accustomed. His cheeks were red, his brow was all crinkled with anger, and the veins stood out at his temples with passion. He locked the door and hurried past me without a word or a look.'

'This aroused my curiosity; so when I went out for a walk in the grounds with my charge, the little so-and-so, I strolled round to that side of the house. There were four windows in a row, three of which were dirty, while the fourth was shuttered up. They were evidently all deserted. As I strolled up and down, glancing at them occasionally, Mr. Rucastle came out to me, looking as merry and jovial as ever.'

'"Ah!" said he, "you must not think me rude if I passed you without a word, my dear young lady. I was preoccupied with business matters."'

'I assured him that I was not offended. "By the way," said I, "you seem to have quite a suite of spare rooms up there, and one of them has the shutters up."'

'"Photography is one of my hobbies," said he. "I have my dark-room up there. But, dear me! What an observant young lady we have come upon. Who would have believed it?"' He spoke in a jesting tone, but there was no jest in his eyes as he looked at me. I read suspicion there, and annoyance, but no jest. Well, Mr.

Holmes, I can tell you now, that NOBODY talks to Miss Hunter like that!'

Holmes and I flicked eyes side-to-side at one another.

'From this moment on I was all fired up. There was something about that suite of rooms that was suspicious. It was not out of curiosity, gentlemen – it was a feeling of duty!'

Sherlock Holmes clapped his hands together and applauded. I had to, sort of, join in.

'Thank you, but it is all in a woman's instinct!' said she, dismissively. 'Anyway, I was keenly on the lookout for any chance to pass the forbidden door. Yesterday, that chance came. Toller and his wife also visit the rooms. Recently, he had been drinking hard and yesterday evening he was very drunk. When I came upstairs he had left a key in the door. I was certain that Mr. and Mrs. Rucastle were downstairs with their unscrupulous child, and so I had an admirable opportunity. I turned the key gently in the lock, opened the door and slipped through.'

'There was a little passage in front of me, unpapered and uncarpeted, which turned a right angle at the farther end. Round this corner were three doors in a line, the first and third were open. They each led into an empty room, dusty and cheerless, with two windows in the one, and one in the other, so thick with dirt that the evening light glimmered dimly through them. The centre door was closed, and across the outside of it had been fastened one of the broad bars of an iron bed, padlocked at one end to a ring in the wall, and fastened at the other with stout cord. The door itself was locked as well, and the key was not there. This barricaded door corresponded clearly with the shuttered window outside but I could see by the gap on the threshold that the room was not in darkness. I suddenly heard steps within the room! I saw a shadow pass backwards and forwards against the threshold slit! A mad, unreasoning terror rose up in me at the sight, Mr. Holmes. My overstrung nerves failed me suddenly, and I turned and ran!'

'Miss Hunter, I was under an impression of your strong resolve,' said Holmes.

So was I!

'Oh, I ran all right!' she said, her voice quavering. 'It was as if some dreadful hand were behind me, clutching at the skirt of my dress! I rushed down the passage, through the door, and straight into the arms of Mr. Rucastle, who was waiting outside.'

'"So," he said, smiling, "it is you, then. I thought it must be when I saw the door open."'

'I told him that I was frightened, nay terrified. He said: "My dear young lady!" over and over, in a very soothing voice whilst caressing my shoulders. But I was on my guard; his manner was a little too coaxing! I told him that I had been foolish, that I had made a mistake. I had been frightened by the loneliness, the eeriness and the dim light.'

'"Only that?" said he, looking at me keenly.'

'"Why, what do you think?" I said in reply.'

'"I lock this door to keep people out; people who have no business here."'

'"If only I had known!" exclaimed I, trying to sound naïve. But then his smile hardened into a grin of rage, and he pulled me close to him strongly, and he glared down at me with the face of a demon!'

Holmes and I sat up. We were on the edge of our seats!

'He said: "You knew precisely what you were doing, Missy! If I catch you again, I'll throw you to the mastiff!"'

'I am not sure what happened next. I must have extricated myself from his grasp and run to my room. I remember nothing until I found myself lying on my bed trembling all over. Then, I thought of you, Mr. Holmes.'

My companion raised his brow luridly. I knew that look, which was a rare one outside the environs of Mother Kelly's. He was imagining Miss Hunter on her bed, all-of-a-tremble. Maybe he was more human than I imagined?

'I could not live there any longer without some sound advice. I was frightened of the house, the servants, my employer and his woman, who kept giving me strange looks. And, on top of it all, there was their loathsome child, who needed no advice on how to pull the wings off butterflies. The boy is a fruit cake. So, I put on my hat and cloak, went down to the post office, which is about half a mile from the house, and then returned, feeling much easier. A horrible doubt crossed my mind as I approached the door, in case the dog might be loose, but I remembered that Toller had drunk himself stupid that evening, and I knew that he was the only one in the household had any influence with the savage creature or would let him out. I slipped in safely, and lay awake for half the night in my joy at the thought of seeing you...'

The great detective inclined his head to her and snuggled down into his chair with the largest, smuggest, most-righteous, puffed-up, piously-hideous smile on his ugly mug that I had ever seen! If only Miss Hunter knew what damage she had done.

'In the morning I had no difficulty in getting leave to come to Winchester, but I was told that I must be back before three o'clock because Mr. and Mrs. Rucastle are going on a visit and will be away all evening and I would be attending to the child. Now, Mr. Holmes, I have told you all my adventures. Please tell me what it means and what I must do.'

Holmes and I had listened spellbound to this extraordinary story. My friend rose now, his hands in his pockets, and an expression of the most profound gravity upon his face.

'Is Toller still drunk?'

'Yes, I heard his wife tell Mrs. Rucastle that she could do nothing with him.'

'That is good. And the Rucastles go out tonight for sure?'

'Yes.'

'Is there a cellar with a good, strong lock?'

'Yes, the wine cellar.'

'You seem to me to have acted all through this matter like a brave and sensible girl, Miss Hunter. Do you think you could perform one more feat? I should not ask it of you if I did not think you a quite exceptional woman.'

'I shall try. What is it?'

'Doctor Watson and I shall be at Copper Beeches by seven o'clock. The Rucastles will be gone by that time, and Toller will, we hope, be incapable. There only remains Mrs. Toller, who might give the alarm. If you could send her into the cellar, on some errand, and then turn the key upon her, you would facilitate matters immensely.'

'I shall do it!'

'Excellent! We shall then look into the affair. Of course there is only one feasible explanation: you have been brought there to impersonate someone, and the real person is imprisoned in this chamber. That is obvious. As to who this prisoner is, I have no doubt that it is the daughter, Miss Alice Rucastle who if I remember right, is said to have gone to America. You were chosen, doubtless, as resembling her in height, figure and the colour of your hair. Hers had been cut off, very possibly in some illness through which she has passed, and so, of course, yours had to be sacrificed also. But you gave me a marvellous opportunity to create a new hairstyle which we have anointed as "The Robert!"'

Miss Hunter burst into spontaneous applause, which, as if by magic, turned other heads in the pub and compelled them to join in. Why? I can only think that they suspected a birthday celebration and may get some free cake. Or maybe they were foreigners? Anyway, the accolade caused The Golden Scissors of Soho to make a deep bow from his waist and ejaculate mock-bashful platitudes. When the room had calmed, he continued with his summing-up, now buoyed up as if he was the Field Marshall of an army just won the war, sauntering up and down the bar, gesticulating left, right and centre.

'Thank you! By a curious chance you came upon her tresses. The man in the road was, undoubtedly, some friend of hers – possibly her fiancé – and no doubt as you wore the girl's dress, and were so like her, he was convinced from your laughter, whenever he saw you, and afterwards from your gesture, that Miss Rucastle was perfectly happy, and that she no longer desired his attentions. The dog is let loose at night to prevent him from endeavouring to communicate with her. So much is fairly clear. The most serious point in the case is the disposition of the child.'

'What on Earth has the brat got to do with it?' I ejaculated (it was my turn).

'My dear Watson, you as a medical man are continually gaining light as to the tendencies of a child by the study of the parents.'

'Habitat, Holmes. Always habitat.'

'Well, don't you see that the converse is equally valid? I have frequently gained my first real insight into the character of parents by studying their children. This child's disposition is abnormally cruel, merely for cruelty's sake, and whether he derives this from his smiling father as I should suspect, or from his mother, it bodes evil for the poor girl who is in their power.'

'I am sure that you are right, Mr. Holmes!' exclaimed our client. 'A thousand things come back to me which make me certain that you have hit it. Oh, let us lose not an instant in bringing help to this poor creature.'

'We must be circumspect, for we are dealing with a very cunning man. We can do nothing until seven o'clock. At that hour we shall be with you, and it will not be long before we solve the mystery.'

Miss Hunter gathered up her things and bade us farewell. Holmes and I sat back down again at the table.

'It is only two o'clock,' said I, staring at my hunter.

'Clearly, it takes an hour to travel from here to Copper Beeches. What are we going to do for the next four hours?'

The great detective bounced upon his seat and rubbed his hands together in keen anticipation.

'Why, we are going to travel there now and make a reconnaissance of the house and its immediate grounds. But first we are going to finish the wine and we are going to each try one of these.'

My companion withdrew the medicine bottle of homemade pills.

'After all, I have cracked this case. It will help to relieve the hours of tedious mediocrity between now and this evening.'

As I divided the wine between us he opened the amber glass bottle, uncorked its wad of cotton wool and jiggled some pills into the palm of his hand. He picked up one 'twixt thumb and forefinger and popped it in his mouth. One swig of Mersault later and it was gone. Then, he offered one up to me.

'No, thank you, Holmes, if it is all the same to you I shall decline. I have no doubt that they give the patient an hallucinogenic view of life. One of us must keep a clear head.'

The amateur chemist trawled air through his incisors, pulled a painfully pinched smirk and raised a buzzing wail of sarcasm from his vocal-chords. Luckily, I had a call of nature. As I walked down the corridor and out of the back door towards the small building that housed the facilities I thought about the situation. He may think that I had a holier-than-thou attitude to drugs but as a doctor who had served in

I knew that I could trust my friend implicitly.

India, Afghanistan and West London I had witnessed the ravages of narcotics on vulnerable people. He had precious little experience of that. Moreover, I never liked to lose any control of my senses, over and above the stimulation of decent booze where I was experienced in my limitations. I returned to the table.

'Are you sure you won't change your mind, Doctor?' said he, with a smirk, shaking the amber bottle at me, like a baby's rattle.

'No, thank you. That sort of thing is fine for you, Holmes – your constitution is used to the damnation of alien chemicals – but my body is as pure as the Virgin Mary's bath water.'

The great detective piqued and then fell onto the table in peals of laughter, slapping the table over and over with his right palm.

'All right, all right, it's not that funny...' said I, but it didn't stop him.

'Oh, yes it is!' he cried, through welling tears in eggy eyes. 'You. In the bath, with the Virgin Mary! What a sight!'

And off he went again into spasms of laughter, taking what seemed like an eternity to regain control. I just watched on, as a doctor as well as a friend, suspecting the pill he had just taken had started to take effect.

'Finish your wine, Watson, whilst I slip another one of these chimps down the hatch.'

I shouted advice, but it was too late. He swallowed the pill and thrust the bottle back into his coat pocket. I drained the glass of delicious Mersault, slightly tart now after it had been sitting, and we headed for the exit to hire a lift to Copper Beeches. The landlord of the inn allowed us to go and find that lift once I had settled the account for luncheon with Holmes blurting out "did you really expect, in your wildest dreams, Watson, for Miss Hunter to take care of the bill?" whilst swaying gently from side-to-side with a wicked grin.

It was five miles of country roads and lanes in a pony and trap to Copper Beeches; five bloody miles of my companion talking incessantly. For once, he was not blathering on about the mystery we were involved in but by a heartfelt assessment of Miss Hunter instead. It turned out that he was attracted to her self-confidence, nay aroused by the way that she spoke, recounting examples of her put-downs to both of us over luncheon and then giggling. He was not in his normal contemplative mood – more playful – no doubt due to the intake of "chimps," as he liked to call them. It was only when I was searching for evidence of my diagnosis by looking into his eyes for pupil dilation that I found myself feeling queasy. At first I put it down to travel sickness but my heart was pumping much faster than usual. I felt giddy, and when I tried to make sense of it by restoring my balance and sitting up straight I found that the interior of the compartment was moving around. Then, when I looked out across the countryside, the land started to elongate in long brushstrokes of brown and green. I realised that I was completely off-colour. Suddenly a wave of emotion coursed through my head and down through my body! Was I going to vomit? No. Was I about to faint? No. I turned to look at my companion.

'I say, Holmes, I feel very, very queer. I don't know why. Maybe I have eaten something?'

'Do you feel a sensation like a gale was blowing through a field of ripe corn?'

'Yes.'

Do you feel as if gigantic waves are crashing over you, engulfing your mind with foamy water, one after the other?'

'Yes!'

'And how do your hands feel??'

'Oh my God, Holmes, I never knew that I had such beautiful knuckles! And my knees – they feel like cannonballs!'

Holmes made a ridiculous face at me by pulling his eyelids down and pushing his nostrils up.

'Do I look like a saddleback pig?'

'I don't know!' I wailed, as he collapsed into laughter. 'Do you know what is the matter with me?'

'You are feeling the effects of one of my chimps' he chirruped. 'Back at the inn one of them accidentally fell into your glass whilst you were visiting the vicar.'

'Ah!' said I, without a care in the world. 'That is why the wine had turned so sour!'

'Sorry, I didn't mean to ruin a decent Mersault. Here, have a another one.'

We laughed as he dispensed another couple of chimps. I didn't care that I was consuming another pill. I didn't give a monkey's arse that he had spiked my wine in the first place. I was feeling bloody marvellous! When we reached the Copper Beeches, there were the trees. They were very impressive and to me they were not copper but a pallet mix of different burnished colours – reds and blues and greens – all wavering in a haze.

'Look, Holmes! Psychedelic trees!'

It was at that moment I realised Holmes had chimped the Mersault. I was flying!

I paid our driver to wait for us at the local public house. Goodness knows what money I gave to him but off he went, happy as Larry. I took little notice of the house itself. I remember it vaguely as being a large country manor house of no particular architectural note in whitewashed stone, but that is all. We had avoided the front driveway and slipped in the side of the property by a small staircase of stone steps that climbed up a bank from the lane. The scullery door was open. We entered the building proper via the kitchen, this section of the house being devoid of servants in the middle of the afternoon. Holmes was leading the way and when we stopped by the doorway into the hall he turned to me wearing the silliest of expressions. His mouth dropped open for a moment as he cocked an ear to listen hard. Then his right hand shot up to his lips as an indication for me to remain silent and, sure enough, I started to laugh. It was his ears – they looked so big, too big for his head! He pointed his finger at me to keep quiet, for now we could hear the faint sound of a wind instrument being played; it was a jolly tune that caught the ear as it wafted through the vast space of the house. Then it stopped, but a few moments later it started up again.

'Ah, Watson! We have a musician amongst us. It must be the child practising the flute. By the way, do you have to dance?'

'Why, pray, do you assume it to be a child? Could it not be the man of the house? And, by the way, I cannot help but dance.'

'Stand still, Watson! No adult would play so poorly and persist in trying to master the phrases unless there was a teacher at hand. I suspect our Miss Hunter is playing her role as governess and compelling the little tyke to play the instrument. Come – I think it is time we took a look for ourselves.'

And before I could say anything more, we had crept up the main staircase, which was big and wide and shiny. My strong, powerful knees were enjoying themselves! At the top of the stairs I felt a wave of euphoria washing all over me, my head racing, the ceiling all of a twirl. My goodness, whatever hallucinogenic compounds Sherlock Holmes had thrown together were having an invigorating effect on me -- I felt blooming marvellous! Holmes grabbed me by the shoulders, his eyes full of mirth mixed with slight concern, and pressed me down to dampen my dancing. Holmes humoured me with a little jig of his own and then we set off along one of the landings, following the sound of the music to a wing where the principal bedrooms of the house were situated. We stopped by a room where the door was ajar and peered in to a nursery-come-playroom; there was a small, blond-haired boy sitting on a chair facing away from us with a music stand in front of him, playing a small flute. He was entertaining a small audience of stuffed figures: an elf, a gnome, two golliwogs, a giraffe and an elephant. There was no sign of our client-governess but a maid stood on guard behind him and each time that he faltered, she would encourage him to start from a certain point in the music, thus repeating the phrases in practice. Holmes and I gave each other a raised brow or two. Then, the great detective spied something further down the landing and set off, prowling slowly. I followed, cat-pouncing from one creaky board to another. On the corner he stopped, as did I, and reached down to pick up a dainty lace handkerchief that had fallen to the floor – a lady's nosegay if ever there was one – and then he cocked an ear to a noise that I had not picked up. He beckoned me to come after him but with his finger pressed to his lips for absolute silence, and we trod carefully through the old house, our knees bent, shifting our body weight with what we thought to be the greatest of skill between each step. He steered a course into a corridor that was lined with wardrobes and it was at this point that I heard some ladies' voices for the first time. I didn't really have the time to ponder recognition before they disappeared and we reached an intricate balustrade barrier of ornate wrought ironwork, spread left to right, where we could go no further. Holmes stopped in his tracks. His body jerked as he caught sight of something important and he dropped down to the floor as quickly as he could. He rolled onto his front. I followed suit and joined him.

We had arrived in the master bedroom suite. This was a grand, vaulted, two-tier construction where the bed chamber was set about fifteen feet below the dressing rooms that we had just crept through. Holmes and I had arrived on the landing at the top. This ended in an iron staircase that snaked down to a very large bed situated below us. Plumb in the middle of that bed was the writhing entwinement of two naked ladies kissing and caressing each other. I recognised one of them, as you would guess immediately, dear adventure-enthusiast, but the other was a stranger to me. I suspected deeply that she was the lady of the house. Whoever she was, she was very beautiful and she moved on Miss Hunter's alabaster physique with smooth elegance, her fingers stroking the folds of her skin with a velvet touch. My eyes were drawn to her high-quality lingerie: a dark green silk (not satin) camisole fringed with black lace propped admirably by her small bare breasts, to a very petite knicker affair, matching green and black, with red thread interline around the muff. Hmmm! This was an expensive set! French, I think. Maybe *Maison Moulin Rouge*? Or was it an Italian *Federeica Quimissimo*? Anyway, I was just thinking to myself that I wouldn't mind being in Miss Hunter's place when my attention drifted over to Holmes. He lay dead still, his eyes moist with disbelief, tinged with a little sadness, probably from the stark realisation that Mother Nature had trampled on his yearnings. I had no such feelings – it had been obvious to me all along that Miss Hunter and Mrs. Rucastle were likely to be sex-positive bum chums – and so all I could do in this difficult situation was to settle in and study their amazingly intimate movements in extremely careful detail!

* * *

It was just after seven that evening, in the light of the setting sun, that Holmes and I walked up to the front door and met Miss Hunter, who had been standing on the doorstep.

'Have you managed it?' asked Holmes, wearing a wry smile.

I was thinking. Yes, all afternoon...This was the entry-level *double-entendre*, the first of many to come I feared.

There was a loud thudding noise came from somewhere downstairs.

'That is Mrs. Toller in the cellar,' said she. 'Her husband lies snoring on the kitchen rug. Here are his keys, which are the duplicates of Mr. Rucastle's.'

'You have done well indeed!' cried Holmes, with enthusiasm. 'And what about the Rucastles?' said he, all innocently knowing full well that we had both watched her employer and her lover depart by carriage over an hour ago.

'Gone,' said Miss Hunter.

'I thought as much…Now lead the way, and we shall soon see the end of this black business.'

We passed up the staircase and, this time, we turned in the opposite direction to that of earlier, Holmes and I exchanging knowing glances all the way. I was feeling much more grounded, the waves of euphoria from the drug now subsided both on frequency and intensity, but my mind was still light and airy – "away with the fairies" as my old Granny Watson would say. The great detective, however, was full of the joys of Spring, despite his ship of desire having been dashed on the coastal rocks of Lesbos. I could only assume that the case-in-hand had re-established itself in the forefront of his mind. I hadn't given it more thought; why should I when I had been helplessly drugged? I was happy to follow our client's delightful *derrière,* wiggling alluringly with every step taken in front of us, even if I had been studying the same, and more, from every angle all afternoon.

We unlocked the first door easily enough, followed on down a passage and found ourselves in front of the barricade which Miss Hunter had described. Holmes cut the cord and removed the transverse bar. But then, when he tried various keys in the door lock, there was no movement. No sound came from within the room, and at the silence Holmes's face clouded over.

'I trust that we are not too late,' said he. 'I think, Miss Hunter, that we had better go in with you. Now, Watson, put your shoulder to it, and we shall see whether we cannot make our way in.'

'Put my shoulder to it?! But Holmes, you could make use of your picks and make short work of that lock.'

'Indeed, if I had remembered to bring them with me.'

'Oh, never mind. Stand back!'

I withdrew the Holland 0.577, grasped its grip firmly and took aim at the lock. As I just said, my mind was still airy and I hadn't thought of the consequences of firing the Manstopper in such close confines.* Luckily, before I could pull the trigger, the long white fingers of my companion came down on mine and stayed me.

'Another time, another place, Watson....'

Holmes barged the door suddenly and it gave at once. I lifted the gun up. It gleamed in the light of the setting sun beaming through the window nearby.

'My, that's a big one...' commented Miss Hunter, huskily.

I lifted the gun and looked at her. 'Thank you, Miss Hunter, but you wouldn't have much use for a big one.' The words had spilled out accidentally in a flashback of Miss Hunter that afternoon – that's what narcotics are for – and she looked very confused, but without further ado we followed Sherlock Holmes into the room. It was empty. There was no furniture save a little pallet bed,

---

* see *The Oranges of Death!* and *The Speckled Band Speculation*

a small table, and a basketful of linen. The skylight above was open, and the prisoner gone.

'There has been some villainy here,' said Holmes; 'this beauty has guessed Miss Hunter's intentions and has carried his victim off.'

'But how?'

'Through the skylight. We shall soon see how he managed it.' He swung himself up onto the roof, as agile as a Greek nymph. For some reason unknown to me, but I suspect Holmes's narcotics, I burst into spontaneous applause. Miss Hunter followed suit.

'You are most kind!' he cried. 'Ah, yes, here is the end of a long light ladder against the eaves. This is how he did it.'

'But it is impossible,' said Miss Hunter, 'the ladder was not there when the Rucastles went away.'

'He has come back and done it. I tell you that he is a clever and dangerous man. In fact, I should not be much surprised if that was his footstep now upon...'

'WHAT THE FUCK IS GOING ON IN HERE?!' asked the fat, burly man now standing in the doorway with a big heavy stick in his hand.

Miss Hunter screamed and jumped back, clapping her hands to her cheeks, with an "Oh, what language, Mr. Rucastle!" I was so appalled by his expletive that I took a pace back and reached inside my jacket to clasp the Manstopper. But Holmes was most dreadfully offended and swooped down from the roof to confront him.

'You foul-mouthed dog!' exclaimed he. And with a quick two-step lunge Holmes punched him square on the nose. 'That is for saying fuck in front of the lady.'

He gave him a second jab and connected once again. 'And that's for saying fuck in front of a doctor. Now, where is your daughter?'

'It is for me to ask *you* that!' he shrieked, reeling backwards and checking his nose for blood. 'You thieves! You villains! I have caught you, have I not? But I am glad that you called me a dog. Now I know how to sort you out! Stay there – I shall be back in a minute!'

He turned and clattered down the stairs as hard as he could go.

'He has gone for the mastiff,' cried Miss Hunter.

'Fear not. It will be no match for my big one,' said I, and showed her the 0.577 Holland again. Miss Hunter gave me the whisp of a rueful smile, as if she knew that I was playing upon her lesbianism.

'We had better close the front door,' cried Holmes, and we rushed down the stairs together. We had hardly reached the hall when we heard the baying of a hound and then a scream of agony, with a horrible worrying sound, which was dreadful to listen to. An elderly man with a red face and shaking limbs came staggering out of a side-door.

'My God!' he cried. 'Some fool has loosed the dog! It has not been fed for two days.'

'Well, it sounds like it has now!' somebody shouted out...maybe yours truly.

'Quick! Quick! Or it will be too late!' cried the sozzled old timer.

Holmes and I rushed out, and round the angle of the house, with Toller hurrying behind us. There was the huge famished brute, its black muzzle buried in

Rucastle's throat, somewhere between chin three and four, while he writhed screaming upon the ground. Blood and sub-cutaneous fat was spurting in all directions. Running up, I pulled out the Manstopper and without a moment's thought I pulled the trigger. Suddenly the world exploded and turned upside down! Only the third shot ever made with this extraordinary feat of engineering and it answered the question that I had asked myself once of what must it be like to fire it when making a forward move – i.e. against the direction of recoil – and I was hurled to one side with Herculean force, as if an invisible giant had swiped me with his big, meaty hand. I hear that it was quite a spectacle as I barrel-rolled through the air and landed on my side with my gun poised as if ready to take a second shot! And when I came to my senses, lying upon the ground fifty yards away, I could see the joyful euphoria from my colleagues that my heroic action had caused; even old Toller was putting his hands together. I could hardly hear them, such was the shockingly loud report of the gunshot, but that didn't matter. I knew that I had done my duty, which was confirmed when I noticed Holmes and Toller separating what was left of the dog from Mr. Rucastle, who was mangled horribly, but living. We laid him upon the drawing-room sofa and, having despatched the sobered-up Toller to find his wife and call for the local surgeon, I did what I could do to relieve his pain. Without the use of the drugs my medical bag and my wrists swelling up from the recoil, I was about as much use as a witch doctor. Then, I had a moment of inspiration.

'I say, Holmes, would you mind passing me that bottle of chimps?'

'Ah!' perked my companion. 'What a very fine idea, Doctor.'

I forced a handful of the pills down the throat of Mr. Rucastle. That would either send him for a journey around the moon and back or to the gates of hell. The door opened and a tall, gaunt woman entered the room.

'This is Mrs. Toller,' commented Miss Hunter, and she introduced us.

'Mr. Rucastle let me out when he came back before he went up to you,' she told us. 'It's a pity you didn't let me know what you were planning, Miss Hunter, for I would have told you that your pains were wasted.'

'Ha!' cried Holmes, triumphantly, looking keenly at her. 'It is clear that Mrs. Toller knows more about this matter than anyone else.'

'Yes, sir, I do, and I am ready enough to tell what I know.'

'Then pray sit down, and let us hear it, for there are several points on which I must confess that I am still in the dark.'

'I will soon make it clear to you,' said she; 'and I'd have done so before now if I could have got out from the cellar. If there's a police-court business over this, you'll remember that I was the one that stood your friend, and that I was Miss Alice's friend too.'

We all mumbled agreement freely, as one does when one is eager to be let in on a secret.

'All right, then. Well, she was never happy at home, Miss Alice wasn't, from the time that her father married again. She was slighted, like, and had no say in anything; but it never really became bad for her until after she met Mr. Fowler at a friend's house. As well as

Holmes didn't care about my injuries. He was handling his Darwinian Instincts!

I could learn, Miss Alice had rights of her own by will, but she was so quiet and patient, she was, that she never said a word about them, but just left everything in Mr. Rucastle's hands. He knew he was safe with her; but when there was a chance of a husband coming forward, who would ask for all that the law could give him, then her father thought it time to put a stop to it. He wanted her to sign a paper so that whether she married or not, he could use her money. When she wouldn't do it, he kept on worrying her until she got brain fever, and for six weeks was at death's door. Then she got better at last, all worn to a shadow, and with her beautiful hair cut off; but that didn't make no change in her young man, and he stuck to her as true as a man could be.'

'Ah,' said Holmes, 'I think that what you have been good enough to tell us makes the matter fairly clear, and that I can deduce all that remains. Mr. Rucastle, then, I presume, took to this system of imprisonment?'

'Yes, sir.'

'And brought Miss Hunter down from London in order to get rid of the disagreeable persistence of Mr. Fowler.'

'That was it, sir.'

'But Mr. Fowler, being a persevering man, as a good seaman should be, blockaded the house, and having met you, succeeded by certain arguments, metallic or otherwise, in convincing you that your interests were the same as his.'

'Mr. Fowler was a very kind-spoken, free-handed gentleman,' said Mrs. Toller serenely.

'And in this way he managed that your good man should have no want of drink, and that the ladder should be ready at the moment when your master had gone out.'

'You have it, sir, just as it happened.'

'I am sure we owe you an apology, Mrs. Toller,' said Holmes, 'for you have certainly cleared up everything which puzzled us. And here comes the country surgeon and Mrs. Rucastle...'

Sure enough, there was the lady of the house, this time presented to us with her clothes on. She carried herself in a calm, relaxed way to where we were assembled and I just caught the tiniest of winks that she sent over to Miss Hunter, which I took to be an invitation to resume intimate liaisons as soon as everyone had all buggered off. Sherlock Holmes picked up the scent immediately.

'I think, Watson, we had best escort Miss Hunter back to Winchester, as it seems to me that our *locus standi* now is rather a questionable one.'

And thus was solved the mystery of the sinister house with the copper beeches, or psychedelic trees as I perceived them when high on chimps. Talking of which... Mr. Rucastle was as high as a kite by the time that we left Copper Beeches, happy as a sambo, so there was something very excellent about the chimps when it came to killing off pain. Maybe Holmes had created something truly wonderful for humanity? Anyway, amazingly enough, Mr. Rucastle survived, but was always a broken man, kept alive solely through the care of his devoted wife. They still lived with their old servants, who probably know so much of Rucastle's past life that he finds it difficult to part from them. Mr. Fowler and Miss Rucastle were married, by special licence, in Southampton the day after their flight, and he is now the holder of a Government appointment in the Island of Mauritius. As to Miss Violet Hunter, my friend Holmes, rather to my disappointment, manifested no further interest in her when once she ceased to be the centre of his problems; at least, that is what he told me, but we know, truly, that it was after she had manifested herself as a lesbian. She is now the head of a private girls' school at Walsall, where I believe that she has met with considerable success. Are we, dear reader, surprised?

As for Holmes and I, we schlepped back up to London Town, with no remuneration for our services and bearing the expenses of the railway, a luncheon and a consultation at St. Thomas's for my wrists, for they had both been fractured by the Manstopper. Funnily enough, my companion suggested a jocular alternative – that I had been over-vigorous with myself whilst leering at the ladies sensualise their many stages of eroticism – but I dismissed his attempt at humour with a swift *deux doigts d'Agincourt*. As the surgeon set my hands in splints and Sherlock Holmes sat by my side reading today's edition of *The Times,* I had a vision of our future adventures together and made a promise to myself to trade off the hefty revolver for something more practical. Sadly, it was a promise that stayed unfulfilled.